Dick King-Smith

The Hodgeheg

Illustrated by Ann Kronheimer

PUFFIN

PUFFIN BOOKS

Published by the Penguin Group
Penguin Books Ltd, 80 Strand, London WC2R 0RL, England
Penguin Group (USA) Inc., 375 Hudson Street, New York, New York 10014, USA
Penguin Group Australia Ltd, 250 Camberwell Road, Camberwell,
Victoria 3124, Australia
Penguin Books Canada Ltd, 10 Alcorn Avenue, Toronto, Ontario, Canada M4V 3B2
Penguin Books Inida (P) Ltd, 11 Community Centre, Panchsheel Park,
New Delhi – 110 017, India
Penguin Group (NZ), cnr Airborne and Rosedale Roads, Albany
Auckland 1310, New Zealand
Penguin Books (South Africa) (Pty) Ltd, 24 Sturdee Avenue, Rosebank, 2196,
South Africa

Penguin Books Ltd, Registered Offices: 80 Strand, London WC2R 0RL, England

www.penguin.com

First published by Hamish Hamilton Ltd 1987
Published in Puffin Books 1989
Reissued in 2003
Published in this edition 2004
This edition produced for The Book People Ltd,
Hall Wood Avenue, Haydock, St Helens, WA11 9UL
1

Text copyright © Dick King-Smith, 1987
Illustrations copyright © Ann Kronheimer, 2003
Introduction copyright © Julia Eccleshare, 2004
All rights reserved

The moral right of the authors and illustrator has been asserted

Set in 15/18½ Perpetua
Made and printed in England by Clays Ltd, St Ives plc

British Library Cataloguing in Publication Data
A CIP catalogue record for this book is available from the British Library

ISBN-13: 978-0-141-33706-7

www.greenpenguin.co.uk

Penguin Books is committed to a sustainable future
for our business, our readers and our planet.
The book in your hands is made from paper
certified by the Forest Stewardship Council.

L Woy

The Hodgeheg

Dick King-Smith served in the Grenadier Guards during the Second World War, and afterwards spent twenty years as a farmer in Gloucestershire, the county of his birth. Many of his stories are inspired by his farming experiences. Later he taught at a village primary school. His first book, *The Fox Busters*, was published in 1978. Since then he has written a great number of children's books, including *The Sheep-Pig* (winner of the Guardian Award and filmed as *Babe*). At the British Book Awards in 1991 he was voted Children's Author of the Year. Dick King-Smith has three children, a large number of grandchildren and several great-grandchildren, and lives in a seventeenth-century cottage only a crow's flight from the house where he was born.

Books by Dick King-Smith

INTRODUCTION

by Julia Eccleshare, Series Editor

How does a hedgehog cross the road? Riskily, as we all know from the number of flattened hedgehogs that litter the roads. But one young hedgehog is determined to change all that.

No one is better than Dick King-Smith at showing the intelligence and resourcefulness of animals. It is he who gave us the chickens who outwit the foxes in *The Fox Busters* and, of course, Babe, the super-intelligent sheepdog – well, pig, actually – in *The Sheep-Pig*. *The Hodgeheg* has all the same hallmarks. Young Victor Maximilian St George (Max for short) has a name that requires a certain amount of living up to. But that's all right. Max is a bright young hedgehog. The death of his Aunt Betty and the following lecture from his parents about road safety sets Max thinking. Humans seem to cross the road safely. How do they do it? For surely, if they can, then so can a hedgehog.

Max's scrutiny of us humans as we cross the road is very funny. What we take for granted seems less straightforward when seen through the eyes of a creature whose head is at foot level. Above all, as Max soon discovers, it shows that what works for people doesn't always work for hedgehogs – or hodgehegs as Max insists on calling them after a dramatic bang on the head muddles up his speech. But by cooperation and common sense, the hedgehogs work together to find a solution to the age-old problem of how to reach the other side of the road ...

The delightful thing about *The Hodgeheg* is that Dick King-Smith gives us a new perspective on the animal world. Hedgehogs are no longer timid creatures with a short lifespan owing to their poor road-crossing skills. Instead, although he always remains firmly an animal, Max and his family behave in remarkably human ways. Mums and dads worry, neighbours can be kind, children are determined, brave – and foolhardy.

The Hodgeheg celebrates ingenuity and individuality and salutes the intelligence and bravery of Victor Maximilian St George, one small hedgehog who became a hero of a hodegheg when he made the First Crossing.

Chapter One

'Your Auntie Betty has copped it,' said Pa Hedgehog to Ma.

'Oh, no!' cried Ma. 'Where?'

'Just down the road. Opposite the newsagent's. Bad place to cross, that.'

'Everywhere's a bad place to cross nowadays,' said Ma. 'The traffic's dreadful. Do you realize, Pa, that's the third this year, and all on my side of the family too. First there was Grandfather, then my second cousin once removed, and now poor old Auntie Betty . . .'

They were sitting in a flowerbed at their home, the garden of Number 5A of a row of semi-detached houses in a suburban street. On the other side of the road was a Park, very popular with local hedgehogs on account of the good hunting it offered. As well as worms and slugs and snails, which they could find in their own gardens, there were special attractions in the Park. Mice lived under the Bandstand, feasting on the crumbs dropped from listeners' sandwiches; frogs dwelt in the Lily Pond, and in the Ornamental Gardens grass snakes slithered through the

shrubbery. All these creatures were regarded as great delicacies by the hedgehogs, and they could never resist the occasional night's sport in the Park. But to reach it, they had to cross the busy road.

'Poor old Auntie Betty,' said Ma again. 'It's a hard life and that's flat.'

'It's a hard death,' said Pa sourly. 'And that's flat too – talk about squashed, the poor old girl was . . .'

'Ssssshhhhh!' said Ma at the sound of approaching footsteps. 'Not in front of the children,' as up trotted four small figures, exact miniatures of their parents except that their spines were still greyish rather than brown. Three of them were little sows, named by Ma, who was fond of flowers, Peony, Pansy and Petunia. Pa had agreed, reluctantly, to these names but had insisted upon his own choice for the fourth, a little boar. Boys, he said, needed noble-sounding names, and the fourth youngster was therefore called Victor Maximilian St George (Max for short).

Almost from the moment his eyes had opened, while his prickles were still soft and rubbery, Max had shown promise of being a bright boy; and by now his eyes, his ears and his wits were all as sharp as his spines.

'What are you talking about, Ma?' he said.

'Nothing,' said Ma hastily.

'You wouldn't be talking about nothing,' said Max, 'or there wouldn't be any point in talking.'

'Don't be cheeky,' said Pa, 'and mind your own business.'

'Well, I suppose it is their business really, Pa, isn't it?' said Ma. 'Or soon will be. They're bound to go exploring outside our garden before long, and we must warn them.'

'You're right,' said Pa. 'Now then, you kids, just you listen to me,' and he proceeded to give his children a long lecture about the problems of road safety for hedgehogs.

Max listened carefully. Then he said, 'Do humans cross the road?'

'I suppose so,' said Pa.

'But they don't get killed?'

'Don't think so,' said Pa. 'Never seen one lying in the road. Which I would have if they did.'

'Well then,' said Max, 'how do they get across safely?'

'You tell me, son. You tell me,' said Pa.

'I will,' said Max. 'I will.'

Chapter Two

Max began his research the very next day. He slipped out of the garden at dusk, ambled along the path by the side wall of Number 5A and crept under the front gate. Immediately, he found himself in a sea of noise.

It was the evening rush-hour and the home-going traffic was at its heaviest.

Cars and motorbikes, buses and lorries thundered past, terrifyingly close it seemed to him, as he crouched outside the gate, and he was confused and dazzled by their lights. The street lamps too lit up the place like day, and Max, nocturnal by nature, made for the darkest spot he could find, in the shadow of a tall litter-bin, and crouched there with hammering heart.

Gradually, he grew a little more accustomed to the din and the glare and, though he dared not move, began to observe the humans, for numbers of pedestrians passed close by him. They were all walking on the narrow road on which he sat, a road raised above the level of the street itself by about the height of a

hedgehog. 'They're safe,' said Max to himself, 'because the noisy monsters aren't allowed up here.'

He looked across the street, and could see that at the far side of it there were other humans, also walking safely on a similar raised road. He did not, however,

happen to see any cross the street.

'But they must cross somewhere,' said Max. 'There must be a place further along the street.'

A part of him, for he was very young,

said that he would find out about that another time and that it would be nice to creep back under the gate to his family. But then another part of him determined to set off to see if he could find this human crossing-place. The street was on a slight slope, and perhaps because of this Max chose to go in the downhill direction. He moved very slowly, keeping close to the outer walls of the front gardens where there was some shadow, and he froze, stock-still, whenever a human passed. No one noticed him.

Soon, the houses gave way to a short row of shops, one of them that very newsagent's opposite which his Great-Aunt Betty had breathed her last, and here his progress was more difficult. The shops were still open, and Max had to choose his moment to make a dash across each brightly lit entrance.

'Phew! This is tiring. Perhaps I should go back home . . .' he said, but then suddenly, not far ahead, he saw what he was seeking. There were humans crossing the street!

Sometimes singly, sometimes in twos and threes, sometimes in quite large groups, they stepped down from the narrow raised road and walked straight across the street with hardly a look to left or right, and stepped up again on the far side, and off they went. And every time that anyone wanted to cross, all the traffic stopped, and waited respectfully until the way was clear again.

This, then, was the magic place! Here
humans could cross in perfect safety! 'If
humans can, why not hedgehogs?'

reasoned Max. But how do people know the exact spot? How do the cars and lorries know when to stop?

Cautiously, he shuffled nearer, keeping close to the wall, until he found himself beside a tall chequered pole on top of which was a glowing orange globe. Across the street, he could see, was a similar pole, and between these two poles the humans walked while the traffic waited.

Biding his time till a moment when there was no one about, Max crept forward to the edge of the raised road and peered down at the surface of the street. It was striped! It was striped, black and white, all the way from one side to the other. This was the secret!

Chapter Three

By now it was quite late. The rush-hour was over. The shops were shut. All was quiet. I'll wait, thought Max, and then when a car or lorry comes along I'll cross in front of it.

Soon he saw something coming. It was a lorry. He was halfway across when he suddenly realized that the lorry hadn't slowed up at all and was almost on top of him, blinding him with its brilliant lights, deafening him with its thunderous roar. It was not going to stop! Lorries only stopped for people – not hedgehogs!

The lorry driver, who, until he was almost upon the crossing, had been quite unaware of the tiny pedestrian, did the only possible thing. With no time to brake or swerve, he steered so as to straddle the little animal. Looking back in his wing-mirror, he saw that it was continuing on its way unhurt, and he grinned and drove on into the night.

The sheer horror of this great monster passing above with its huge wheels on either side of him threw Max into a blind panic, and he made for the end of the

crossing as fast as his legs would carry him. He did not see the cyclist silently pedalling along close to the kerb and the cyclist did not see him until the last moment. Feverishly the man twisted his handlebars, and the front wheel of the bicycle, suddenly wrenched round, caught Max on the rump and catapulted him head first into the face of the kerbstone.

The next thing that Max recalled was crawling painfully under his own front gate. Somehow he had managed to come

back over the zebra crossing. He had
known nothing of the concern of the
cyclist, who had dismounted, peered at
what looked like a small dead hedgehog,
sighed and pedalled sadly away. He
remembered nothing of his journey
home, wobbling dazedly along on the now
deserted pavement, guided only by his
sense of smell. All he knew was that he
had an awful headache.

The family had crowded round him on
his return, all talking at once.

'Where have you been all this time?'
asked Ma.

'Are you all right, son?' asked Pa.

'Did you cross the road?' they both said,
and Peony, Pansy and Petunia echoed,
'Did you? Did you? Did you?'

For a while Max did not reply. His thoughts were muddled, and when he did speak, his words were muddled too.

'I got a head on the bump,' he said slowly.

The family looked at one another.

'Something bot me on the hittom,' said Max, 'and then I headed my bang. My ache bads headly.'

'But did you cross the road?' cried his sisters.

'Yes,' said Max wearily. 'I hound where the fumans cross over, but –'

'But the traffic only stops if you're a human?' interrupted Pa.

'Yes,' said Max. '*Not* if you're a hodgeheg.'

Chapter Four

'D'you suppose he'll be all right?' said Ma anxiously.

It was dawn, and they were about to retire for the day. The children were already asleep in a thick bed of fallen leaves.

'I should hope so,' said Pa. '"Hodgeheg" indeed! His brains are scrambled.'

Max slept the clock round and halfway round again; he did not stir till the evening of the following day. The shock had sent him into a kind of short, early hibernation.

When at last he woke, his sisters rushed to nuzzle at his nose (the safest nuzzling place for hedgehogs) with squeaks of concern, and his parents left their snail-hunting and came trotting up.

'How are you feeling, dear?' said Ma.

Max considered this. His headache was almost gone, and he was thinking straight, but his speech, he found, would still not behave properly.

'I'm a bet bitter, thanks,' he said.

'You had a nasty knock,' said Pa.

'You need rest,' said Ma. 'Why not get

back into bed? We will bring you some nice slugs.'

'I don't want to bed into get,' said Max. 'I feel quite wake awide. In fact, I feel like walking for a go.'

Pa took a moment to work this one out. Then he said firmly, 'You're not going anywhere, son, d'you hear me? You stay home in the garden for a while. Get your strength back, understand?'

'Yes, Pa,' said Max. 'I'll say what you do.' And he did do what Pa had said, for a week or more.

Peony, Pansy and Petunia fussed over their brother. They brought him the fattest, slimiest slugs they could find, and encouraged him to play their favourite game, Hide-and-Seek. However, this didn't work. When they hid, Max forgot to go and look for them; and when it was his turn, he forgot to go and hide, so busy was he thinking about the business of road-crossing. The girls would count to thirty with their eyes shut, but when they opened them, Max would still be sitting there thinking. Striped bits were no good – he didn't intend trying that again – but maybe, he thought, there were other methods.

His determination to find out was increased when Pa came back early one morning from a visit to the Park, with more bad news. Max overheard him telling Ma.

'Another one gone,' Pa said.

'Not a relation?' said Ma fearfully.

'No,' said Pa. 'Chap from Number 9A just up the road, I didn't know him well, you understand, but he always seemed a decent sort of hog. He was crossing just in front of me, not ten minutes ago. Misjudged it. Motorbike got him. Leaves a wife and six kids.'

That evening Max waited until he was sure that Pa was out of the way, in the garden of Number 5B. The people in 5A always put out bread and milk for Max's

family, but the people in 5B often provided something much better for their hedgehogs — tinned dog food.

Every evening, Pa crept through the dividing hedge to see if he could nick a saucerful of Munchimeat before his neighbour woke from the day's sleep.

'Ma,' said Max, 'I'm walking for a go.'

Ma was quick at translating by now.

'Did Pa say you could go?' she said.

'No,' said Max, 'but he couldn't say I didn't,' and before Ma could do anything he trotted off along the garden path.

'Oh, Max!' called Ma. 'Are you sure you'll be all right?'

'Yes, of course,' said Max. 'I'll be quite KO.'

Once outside the garden gate he turned left and set off up the road, in the opposite direction to his previous effort. By now he was used to the noise and the

brightness, and confident that he was safe
from traffic as long as he did not step
down into the road. When a human
passed, he stood still. The creatures did
not notice you, he found, if you did not
move.

He trotted on, past the garden of
Number 9A with its widow and six kids,
until the row of houses ended and a high

factory wall began, so high that he would
not have been able to read the notice on it
beside the factory entrance: Max Speed 5
mph it said.

Max kept going (a good deal more
slowly than this), and then suddenly, once
again, he saw not far ahead what he was
seeking. Again, there were people crossing
the street!

This time they did not go in ones and twos at random, but waited all together and then, at some signal he supposed, crossed at the same time. Max drew nearer, until he could hear at intervals a high, rapid peep-peep-peeping noise, at the sound of which the traffic stopped and the people walked over in safety.

Creeping closer still, tight up against the wall, he finally reached the crossing-place, and now he could see this new magic method. The bunch of humans stood and watched, just above their heads, a picture of a little red man standing quite still. The people stood quite still.

Then suddenly the little red man disappeared and underneath him

there was a
picture of a little
green man,
walking, swinging
his arms. The
people walked,
swinging their arms, while the
high, rapid peep-peep-peeping
noise warned the traffic not to
move.

Max sat and watched for
quite a long time, fascinated
by the red man and the green
man. He rather wished they
could have been a red
hedgehog and a green
hedgehog, but that was not
really important, as long

as hedgehogs could cross here safely. That was all he had to prove, and the sooner the better.

He edged forward, until he was just behind the waiting humans, and watched tensely for the little green man to walk.

Chapter Five

What Max had not bargained for, when
the bunch of people moved off at the
peep-peep-peeping of the little green
man, was that another bunch would be
coming towards him from the other side
of the street. So that when he was about
halfway across, hurrying along at the heels
of one crowd, he was suddenly confronted

by another. He dodged about in a forest of
legs, in great danger of being stepped on.
No one seemed to notice his small shape
and, indeed, he was kicked by a large foot
and rolled backwards.

Picking himself up, he looked across
and found to his horror that the green

man was gone and the red man had
reappeared. Frantically, Max ran on as the
traffic began to move, and reached the far
side just in front of a great wheel that
almost brushed his backside. The shock of
so narrow an escape made him roll up,
and for some time he lay in the gutter

whilst above his head the humans stepped on to or off the pavement and the noisy green man and the silent red man lit up in turn.

After a while there seemed to be fewer people about, and Max uncurled and climbed over the kerb. He turned right and set off in the direction of home. How to re-cross the street was something he had not yet worked out, but in his experience neither striped bits nor red and green men were the answer.

As usual he kept close to the wall at the inner edge of the pavement, a wall that presently gave place to iron railings. These were wide enough apart for even the largest hedgehog to pass between. Max slipped through. In the light of a full moon he could see before him a wide stretch of grass and he ran across it until the noise and stink of the traffic were left behind.

'Am I where?' said Max, looking round him. His nose told him of

the scent of flowers (in the Ornamental Gardens), his eyes told him of a strange-shaped building (the Bandstand), and his ears told him of the sound of splashing water (as the fountain spouted endlessly in the Lily Pond).

Of course! This was the place that Pa had told them all about! This was the Park!

'Hip, hip, roohay!' cried Max to the moon, and away he ran.

For the next few hours, he trotted busily about the Park, shoving his snout into everything. Like most children, he

was not
only nosy
but noisy
too, and at
the sound of
his coming the
mice scuttled under the
Bandstand, the snakes slid away through
the Ornamental Gardens and the frogs
plopped into the safe depths of the Lily
Pond. Max caught
nothing.

At last he began to feel rather tired and to think how nice it would be to go home to bed. But which way was home?

Max considered this, and came to the unhappy conclusion that he was lost. Just then he saw, not far away, a hedgehog crossing the path, a large hedgehog, a Pa-sized hedgehog! What luck! Pa had crossed the street to find him! He ran forward, but when he reached the animal he found it was a complete stranger.

'Oh,' said Max, 'I peg your bardon. I thought you were a different hodgeheg.'

The stranger looked curiously at him. 'Are you feeling all right?' he said.

'Yes, thanks,' said Max. 'Trouble is, I go to want home. But I won't know the day.'

'You mean . . . you don't know the
way?'

'Yes.'

'Well, where do you live?' asked the
strange hedgehog.

'Number 5A.'

'Indeed? Well now, listen carefully,
young fellow. Go up this path – it will

take you back to the street – and a little way along you'll see a strange sort of house that humans use. It's a tall house, just big enough for one human to stand up in, and it has windows on three sides and it's bright red. If you cross there, you'll fetch up right by your own front gate. OK?'

'KO,' said Max, 'and thanks.'

As soon as he was through the Park railings, he saw the tall, red house. He trotted up close to it. It was lit up, and sure enough there was a human inside it. He was holding something to his ear and Max could see that his lips were moving. How odd, thought Max, moving very close now, he's standing in there talking to himself!

At that instant the man put down the receiver and pushed open the door of the telephone booth, a door designed to clear the pavement by about an inch, the perfect height for giving an inquisitive young hedgehog – for the second time in his short life – a tremendous bang on the head.

Chapter Six

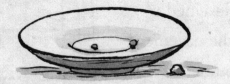

Meanwhile, back at Number 5A, Pa
had had a bonanza. Sneaking next door
and finding a full saucer of dog food and
no sign of his neighbour, he had scoffed
the lot.

He came staggering back, very full of
himself and Munchimeat, and fell into a
deep, bloated sleep.

Ma woke him just before dawn. 'Pa,' she said. 'Wake up. Max hasn't come back.'

Pa opened his eyes and saw her worried face and the three smaller but equally worried faces of Peony, Pansy and Petunia.

'He's been gone all night,' said Ma. 'Oh,

Pa, do you think something's happened to him?'

Pa got to his feet. 'I don't know,' he said, 'but don't fret, Ma. I'll find him.'

'But he could be anywhere. How are you going to know where to look?' Before Pa could answer, he heard a strange voice, coming from the hedge that divided 5A and 5B.

'Excuse me,' said the strange voice, and out poked the head of their neighbour. Pa bristled, his spines standing on end. It's that Munchimeat, he thought. He's found his empty saucer and he's going to cut up rough about it. Well I can play rough too. I don't like the look of him anyway and if he wants a fight, he can have one. We'll soon see who's the better hog.

But before he could think of anything to say, the hedgehog from 5B came out of the hedge and said again, 'Excuse me.'

'Well?' said Pa.

'I couldn't help overhearing what you were saying.'

'Family matter,' growled Pa.

'Exactly. You're worried about your little lad.'

'Oh!' cried Ma. 'Have you seen him?'

'Yes, I have. At least I met a young chap in the Park who said he was lost and looking for the way back to 5A. Unless of course it was a 5A in some other street.'

'Did you notice anything . . . different about him?' asked Ma quickly.

The neighbour looked a trifle embarrassed.

'Well, yes,' he said, 'now that you mention it. He seemed to be having a little bit of difficulty with his speech – muddled some of his words now and then.'

'Like "hodgeheg"?'

'Yes.'

'That's our Max!' cried Ma.

'Was he all right?' asked Pa. 'Not hurt or anything?'

'No, he was fine. I told him the best way to go home. He'll be along soon, I'm sure. Try not to worry.'

Pa cleared his throat awkwardly. His neighbour's kindness greatly added to his feelings of guilt.

'It's very decent of you,' he said.

'Glad to help. That's what neighbours are for.'

'Can we offer you something?' said Ma. 'Some bread and milk?'

'Oh, no thanks,' said the neighbour. 'I had a pretty good night's hunting in the Park. Just as well, because when I got home I found that something had eaten all my Munchimeat.' He looked directly at

Pa, and his eyes were twinkling. 'It was a cat, I expect,' he said, and back through the hedge he went.

'Wasn't that nice of him!' said Ma, and Peony, Pansy and Petunia chanted, 'Nice! Nice! Nice!'

Pa grunted. A part of him thought that he should confess his sin to his neighbour. But then another part of him, for he was very worldly-wise, thought that least said was soonest mended. Life was full enough of headaches without inviting any extra ones.

The same thought occurred to Max when at last he came to his senses. The door of the telephone booth had knocked him out cold, and the neighbour from 5B had not noticed the still, small figure as he hurried to cross the deserted street before the morning rush-hour began.

Oh, thought Max, has any hedgehog ever had a more horrible headache? The last bang I got made me talk a bit funny and I expect this one's made things even worse. I'd better try saying something.

'Oh,' said Max, 'has any hedgehog ever had a more horrible headache?' Max considered this. It sounded fine. Suddenly he felt fine. Even the ache already felt much less.

'My name,' he said softly, 'is Victor Maximilian St George, and,' (he said more loudly), 'I have three sisters called Peony, Pansy and Petunia and I live with Pa and Ma at Number 5A, and,' (he shouted at the top of his voice), 'I am a very lucky

HEDGEHOG!' and without thinking, without listening, without a single glance to left or to right, he dashed across the street, straight in front of the first of that morning's vehicles – the milk van.

The noise that followed was enough to wake the whole street.

First there was a screech as the milkman braked and swerved, and then came the shattering sound of

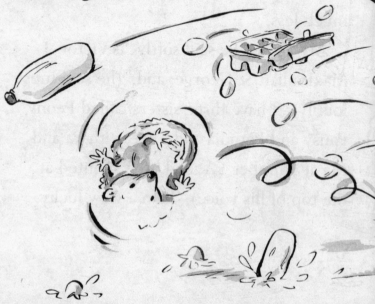

dozens and dozens of bottles smashing.
Lastly came the sound of the milkman's
voice cursing every hedgehog ever born,
as he danced with rage in a sea of Gold
Top and Silver Top, of Semi-skimmed and
Skimmed, of Orange Squash and
Grapefruit Juice and Fresh Farm
Eggs.

Ma and Pa had sent the girls to bed and were waiting up in the growing light of dawn. They were crouching side by side listening, when suddenly the dreadful racket burst upon their ears.

'Sounds like something's got run over,' said Pa heavily. 'Brace yourself, old lady. It could be our Max.'

Ma buried her head and rolled herself into a ball of misery.

At that moment they heard a cheery voice.

'Now, now!' it said. 'What's all the fuss about? There's no point in crying over spilt milk!'

Chapter Seven

What a happy scene of grunting, snuffling, squeaking joy there was in the garden of 5A as the girls were woken to be told the good news! And what a jolly crunching of snails there was as the family celebrated with a feast!

After it all, Max slept heavily, and by evening, when he reappeared, the

neighbour had come through the hedge
twice, once to enquire if Max was back
and again to ask if he was quite well.

At first Ma and Pa felt a little
uncomfortable at these visits, Ma because
she knew what Pa had done, Pa because
he knew that the neighbour knew. But the
matter was not mentioned.

They had been wrong, they found, in

supposing that a family of hedgehogs lived next door. The neighbour had never married and, as elderly bachelors often are, he was rather lonely and very fond of children. He had already invited Peony, Pansy and Petunia to come and play in his garden whenever they liked and, seeing that they were not sure how to address him, had asked them to call him 'Uncle'.

'Uncle what?' they said.

The neighbour scratched his head thoughtfully with his hindfoot.

'Let's see now,' he said. 'I live in the garden of Number 5B. How about "Uncle B"?'

After dark the family were worm-hunting on the lawn when there was a rustling in the dividing hedge and the three girls ran towards it, crying, 'Uncle B! Uncle B! Uncle B!'

'Who's Uncle B?' asked Max.

'Our next-door neighbour,' said Ma. 'That's what the girls call him. They've been playing in his garden.'

'But, Pa,' said Max, 'I thought you couldn't stick him?'

Pa was saved from replying by the approach of Uncle B, and now Max recognized him.

'Oh hello, sir,' he said politely. 'You're the gentlehog I met in the Park. Thank you very much for your help.'

'Don't mention it, Max,' said Uncle B. 'Glad to hear from your parents that you're, um, totally recovered.'

'You should stay in the garden, son,' said Pa. 'You're safe in here.'

Max considered this. He had no intention of giving up his research. The neighbour had helped him once. Maybe he could do so again. As if reading his thoughts, Uncle B said, 'Well, I must be running along now. Any time you feel like having a chat, Max, you just pop over.'

The next night Max popped over.

'Hello, young fellow,' said Uncle B. 'Have some Munchimeat. They always give me more than I can manage.'

'No, thanks. It's your advice I need,' said

Max, getting straight to the point.

'Shoot,' said Uncle B.

He listened carefully while Max told
him everything that had happened so far
in his efforts to find a safe hedgehog-

crossing. 'I must say,' he said when Max had finished, 'I admire your spirit. And your ambition. Finding a really safe way to cross roads would benefit the whole of hedgehogkind. But the two methods that humans use don't seem to be suitable for us. No better, it appears from your experiences, than the old time-honoured way – look right, look left, look right again, before going across. One thing strikes me, however.' Uncle B paused.

'What's that, Uncle B?'

'All your research so far has been at night-time because hedgehogs are nocturnal. But humans aren't. They don't see at all well at night, which is why they keep on clobbering us. Now if you could only find a place to cross in broad daylight, then at least they could see us coming. It might pay us to change our habits. Better to lose your sleep than your life, that's what I say.'

'Well,' said Max, 'I suppose that either of the two ways I've tried would work in daylight too. Trouble is with either of them, you've got to get across so quickly. Now if only there was a human who could stop the traffic and make absolutely sure it didn't move till you were safely over.'

'There are humans like that,' said Uncle B. 'I saw one once, when I was out during the day – not something I often do. He was a big man dressed in blue, with a tall domed hat on his head. He just held up his hand and everything stopped while some small humans crossed the street.

Once they were safely on the other side, he waved the traffic on again.'

Max pondered this. 'So,' he said, 'there might be lots and lots of small humans who have to cross the street by day?'

Uncle B nodded.

'And the big humans,' Max continued, 'would worry about the small ones getting across safely?'

'Oh, yes. Just like hedgehogs.'

'So there simply must be a special perfectly safe daytime crossing-place for small humans — now where on earth could that be?'

'You tell me, Max. You tell me,' said Uncle B.

'I will,' said Max. '*I will!*'

Chapter Eight

Max could hardly wait for the next dawn. Something inside him said that today he would at last be successful in his quest, and outside him every one of his five thousand spines tingled with excitement. The more he thought of his conversation with Uncle B, the more he felt convinced that the answer to the problem lay with

the small humans. Their crossing-place
must be the safest. Follow them and he
would find it.

He waited until the family were fast
asleep, and then, blinking in the
unaccustomed sunlight, he went along the
path by the side wall of Number 5A to the
front gate. He did not go under it but
waited, watching beneath it. Already he
had learned that you could tell the age of
humans from the size of their feet, and he
settled himself to wait patiently until a
pair of small ones should come past.
When at last they did, he was about to go
out and follow but then another pair went
by and then several pairs, and then, as the
pavement filled up with school-going
children, dozens and dozens of small feet

went walking, dancing, skipping, hopping
past his gate.

All of them were going in the same
direction, to his left, up the road, which
would take them, he knew, to the end of

the row of houses and past the factory to
the red man and the green man. Was that,
after all, where all small humans crossed?
He must follow, he must know for sure.

At last, when it seemed to him that no

more feet were coming, Max crept under his gate and set out. Some way ahead he could see the tail of the procession and he hurried after. He had passed the last of the houses and reached the factory entrance when he saw that the crowd was taking no notice of the changing red and green men. They were going to a spot further on. And they were crossing over the road there!

He ran on (under the notice 'Max Speed 5 mph'– and he wasn't far short of it) until he was close enough to see exactly what was going on. And oh, what a scene it was!

'Oh, what a scene it was!' he told the family and Uncle B that evening. 'There was this great big human (it was a female, I could tell by the voice) and she was dressed in a long white coat and she had a black cap with a peak and she carried a long pole and on the top of the pole was a big white round disc with an orange rim and black marks on it – a magic wand it must have been, because she walked out into the middle of the street and held it up and all the traffic stopped dead!'

He paused for breath.

'Then what?' said Pa.

'Then all the small humans went across and the great big female just stood there until the very last one reached the other side safely. And all that time everything stood absolutely still. Buses, lorries, cars, motorbikes, not one of them dared move an inch for fear of the great female and her magic wand!'

'Where did the small humans go, Max?' asked Uncle B.

'Into a huge building,' said Max. 'And I hid myself and watched all day, and at the end of the afternoon they all came out of the building again and there was the great female waiting for them, in her white coat and her black hat, and she waved her wand again and saw them all safely back across. I tell you, it's the ideal place for us – the huge building's right next to the Park. Nothing would ever dare touch us if we were under the protection of that great powerful human!'

'But I don't want to spend the daytime in the Park,' said Pa. 'Setting out in the

morning and coming back in the afternoon — that's no good to me. I need a good day's sleep.'

'You could still get that, old hog,' said Uncle B. 'You could go over in the morning, find a nice place to lie up — under the Bandstand, let's say — get your eight hours, have a good night's hunting, and come back the following morning. Do it once a week perhaps. You could take your wife and the girls — it'd make a nice outing.'

'Oh please, Pa! Please! Please!' cried Peony, Pansy and Petunia.

Pa considered this. 'One of us ought to try it first. See if it works,' he said. 'And if anyone's going, it's me.'

'Not without me,' said Ma stoutly.

'Why not let me go,' said Uncle B.
'After all, I've had a good long life and if
anything goes wrong, there'll be no one
to miss me.'

'Oh yes there will!' cried all the family.

'Look,' said Max. 'You don't know which way to go, how to get there, where exactly it is. None of you can go without me.'

'Well, then,' said Ma, 'why don't we all go?'

Chapter Nine

Very early the following morning seven spiny shapes emerged from under the front gates of Numbers 5A and 5B. They set off up the road, passing garden after garden from many of which (like 9B) a hedgehog had set out on a journey to the Park, never to return. If only they could succeed today! Henceforth the street

would be forever safe for all
hedgehogkind!

They passed the factory and the
automatic crossing with its little red and
green men, and came at last to the spot
where Max had seen the great female
with the magic wand. Opposite them
across the street, the school clock showed

six. The hedgehogs concealed themselves
in a doorway and settled down to wait.

At a quarter past eight, the lollipop lady
arrived. Even the earliest children never
appeared before half-past, but she liked to
be in good time. She stood stamping her
large feet, for it was a crisp morning. She
smoothed down her long white coat. She

settled her black cap firmly. Then, grasping her staff of office, its circular disc bearing the words 'Caution. Children crossing', she stood at attention at the kerbside, ready for the firstcomers, while the early rush-hour traffic roared past.

Never, for the rest of her life, did the lollipop lady forget the sight that now met her eyes. Coming along the pavement towards her were seven hedgehogs in single file.

'Surely you're not going to school?' said the lollipop lady when they reached her.

The noise she made meant nothing to Max, but he advanced to the edge of the kerb, his nose pointing eagerly across the street, the others lined up behind him.

'We wish to go to the Park,' he said. 'Kindly stop the traffic.' The noise he made meant nothing to the lollipop lady, but his intention was as clear as the day. Raising her magic wand on high, the great female strode into the middle of the street and at the sight of her the traffic meekly halted.

Then, before the astonished eyes of those fortunate enough to witness this historic occasion, there walked across the street a slow, solemn dignified procession – of hedgehogs.

At the rear was Uncle B, shepherding before him Peony, Pansy and Petunia. In front of them was Ma. In front of her was Pa. But at the head of the file there marched that pioneer of road safety, Victor Maximilian St George, a name to be remembered forever by hedgehogs the world over.

*

'Tell us the story of the First Crossing, Mummy,' little hedgehogs would plead at bedtime, and then they would listen, enthralled, to the tale of Max, the hedgehog who became a hodgeheg who became a hero. Always the mothers ended with the same words: '. . . and they all crossed happily ever after!'

Read more in Puffin

For complete information about books available from Puffin – and Penguin – and how to order them, contact us at the appropriate address below. Please note that for copyright reasons the selection of books varies from country to country.

www.puffin.co.uk

In the United Kingdom: Please write to Dept EP, Penguin Books Ltd, Bath Road, Harmondsworth, West Drayton, Middlesex UB7 ODA

In the United States: Please write to Penguin Putnam Inc., P.O. Box 12289, Dept B, Newark, New Jersey 07101–5289 or call 1–800–788–6262

In Canada: Please write to Penguin Books Canada Ltd, 10 Alcorn Avenue, Suite 300, Toronto, Ontario M4V 3B2

In Australia: Please write to Penguin Books Australia Ltd, P.O. Box 257, Ringwood, Victoria 3134

In New Zealand: Please write to Penguin Books (NZ) Ltd, Private Bag 102902, North Shore Mail Centre, Auckland 10

In India: Please write to Penguin Books India Pvt Ltd, 11 Panscheel Shopping Centre, Panscheel Park, New Delhi 110 017

In the Netherlands: Please write to Penguin Books Netherlands bv, Postbus 3507, NL–1001 AH Amsterdam

In Germany: Please write to Penguin Books Deutschland GmbH, Metzlerstrasse 26, 60594 Frankfurt am Main

In Spain: Please write to Penguin Books S. A., Bravo Murillo 19, 1° B, 28015 Madrid

In Italy: Please write to Penguin Italia s.r.l., Via Felice Casati 20, I–20124 Milano

In France: Please write to Penguin France S. A., 17 rue Lejeune, F–31000 Toulouse

In Japan: Please write to Penguin Books Japan, Ishikiribashi Building, 2–5–4, Suido, Bunkyo-ku, Tokyo 112

In South Africa: Please write to Longman Penguin Southern Africa (Pty) Ltd, Private Bag X08, Bertsham 2013